How Big is Your Brave?

by Ruth Soukup

Illustrated by Alison Friend

To my daughters, Maggie & Annie.
May you always remember to dream big, work hard, and Do It Scared.
—RS

For AA – Everything is possible!
—AF

ZONDERKIDZ

How Big is Your Brave?
Copyright © 2020 by Ruth Soukup
Illustrations © 2020 by Alison Friend

Requests for information should be addressed to:

Zonderkidz, 3900 Sparks Drive SE, Grand Rapids, Michigan 49546

Hardcover ISBN 978-0-310-76660-5

Ebook ISBN 978-0-310-76663-6

Editor: Barbara Herndon

Art direction and design: Kris Nelson/StoryLook Design

Printed in China

20 21 22 23 24 / DSC / 20 19 18 17 16 15 14 13 12 11 10 9 8 7 6 5 4 3 2 1

Zippy flopped back and looked up at the stars and the deep, dark sky

be to hop in a rocket and blast off for outer space. *Vrrrrrooooom!*

"Not me," said her brother, Gus. "I could never go so far from my garden. But when *you* blast off, I'll cheer you on."

The next day, as Zippy and Gus went into town, they passed by a crowd gathered around a sign:

SPACE CAMP
Launch Your Own Rocket Ship.
Win Ribbons for Best-in-Space.

Zippy's heart soared. "Ooh, that would be fun," she said.

"Sign up," Gus urged. Zippy shook her ears. "No, no, no, no," she said. "Look at all those big critters. I can't compete with them."

"Going to space is your big dream," Gus said. "Wouldn't Space Camp be a good step—like planting the first seed in a garden?"

"Maybe," Zippy said. "But it looks way too scary."

Back home, Zippy couldn't stop thinking about Space Camp. She really wanted to go, but when she thought of those big, smart-looking critters signing up, her whiskers shook. Would they laugh at her? Would they think a little bunny had no business aiming for the stars?

Zippy looked up. The first stars were just beginning to shine in the wide sky. Oh, how she wished to someday soar near them.

YOUR WHY MUST BE BIGGER

Suddenly Zippy remembered something her grandma used to say—that your WHY must be bigger than your fear. She stood up and brushed the dirt from her paws. She'd made her decision. If she wanted to go to space, she had to learn everything she could. Scared or not, she belonged at Space Camp.

HAN YOUR FEAR.

Zippy's whiskers trembled when she arrived for the first day of camp. She huddled next to her mom as the other campers ran about talking and playing. "I keep telling myself to be brave," she whispered. "But I'm still scared."

Mom gave Zippy's back a pat. "Being brave doesn't mean you're never scared," she said. "Sometimes, courage means taking an action, even when you feel afraid."

Zippy watched as two campers began to build a model of the solar system. She took a deep breath and hopped over to them.

"I can make Saturn," she offered in a squeaky voice. As she molded clay into a ball and cut out paper rings, Zippy's nervousness vanished.

ACTION IS THE ANTIDOTE TO FEAR.

Every morning, the campers learned about space and stars and planets and astronauts. Every afternoon, they worked on their rocket ships. As her rocket ship grew, so did Zippy's confidence.

Before long, she was answering questions, asking for help, and making new friends.

At home, Zippy read books about famous astronauts.

"Space Camp seems like a lot of work," Gus remarked.

"I'm just reading these for fun," Zippy said. "Once camp is over, I'm starting a space club with two of my new friends."

"Then will you be a real astronaut?" Gus wondered.

Zippy smiled. "Not yet. Becoming an astronaut takes a lot of studying and hard work," she explained. "That's why we're forming the club. We're going to learn as much as we can together. Our camp counselor says it will be easier to keep our eyes on the stars if we help each other. She says it is something called accountability."

EVERYONE NEEDS ACCOUNTABILITY.

After Space Camp, Zippy carried her rocket ship home to show Gus.
He was busy setting up a juice stand to test out his latest concoctions.

"Wow! Your rocket ship sparkles like the sun,"
Gus said as he swooped the rocket through the air.
"Careful!" said Zippy.
Suddenly, Gus tripped and—

CRASH!
Splash!

Zippy's rocket ship landed in the dirt, crumpled and covered with juice.
"I'm sorry!" Gus said.
"My perfect rocket ship!" Zippy cried. "It's ruined!"

At dinner, Zippy nibbled on lettuce and looked sadly at her cracked, messy rocket ship. Mom offered to help her fix it. Dad did too. Gus volunteered to repaint it.

Zippy shook her ears. "There's no point. I'm not going to Launch Day tomorrow," she said. "I'm done with Space Camp."

Dad looked over at the rocket. "Such a beautiful creation, and now it's broken," he said. "Unfortunately, we can't change that."

Zippy slumped. "No kidding."

"But you can change one thing," Dad continued. "And that's what you're going to do about it. Bad things happen sometimes, and when they happen to you, only you can decide how to react. You can choose to give up or choose to keep going. It's all up to you."

Zippy nodded. She knew what she had to do.

Zippy curled up in her room next to her books.
She looked at all the pictures of astronauts who
came before her.

*I guess they didn't give up easily, so I won't
either,* she thought. *Time to get to work.*

THE ONLY THING YOU CAN
CONTROL IS YOU.

Zippy found some thick paper and created new fins for her rocket ship.

"You could paint it silver," Dad suggested. "That would add some sparkle to your ship."

Zippy munched on a carrot. "I have another idea," she said.

Zippy arrived for Launch Day, nervous but excited. She was happy to see her Space Camp friends and admire their rocket ships.

They were all beautiful. But Zippy's swirling purple-and-orange design really stood out.

"It's lovely," the teacher said. "Were you inspired by the colors of Jupiter?"

Zippy smiled at Gus. "No, I was thinking of my brother's garden. He grows the best beets and carrots."

"Well, that explains the name," the teacher said with a laugh.

LAUNCH DAY

The critters launched their rocket ships, one by one.
Zippy's Veggie Vrrrooom sailed to second place.
And thanks to her unique paint job, she received
a blue ribbon for the most creative design.

SPACE CAMP
MOST
★ CREATIVE ★
Rocket ship
DESIGN

That evening, Zippy and Gus flopped back and looked up at the stars.

"Do you still want to hop in a rocket ship and blast off for outer space someday?" Gus asked.

"More than ever," Zippy said. "I wish you would come with me."

"Only if the rocket ship has a garden," Gus said.

"Great idea," said Zippy. "Astronauts need lots of food in space."